A blessing especially for

_____

A Blessing for
SUMMER'S
CHILD

Words by PETER
HINCKLEY

BUSHEL
& PECK
BOOKS

$\mathcal{D}$earest child of
summer, may the
wonder of your season
always live within you.

*M*ay each day bring the smile of the nodding sunflower...

...the sweetness of the sunny berry...

. . . and the kiss of the evening rain.

$\mathcal{M}$ay the summer wind be
ever at your back . . .

...the sun warm
upon your face...

. . . and the grass soft
beneath your feet.

$\mathcal{M}$ay you soar like
the seabird on
life's perfect days . . .

... run like the deer in its shady forests ...

... bend like the willow
when its winds blow ...

. . . and always have the
strength of the ancient
oak, who knows that no
storm lasts forever.

May you always be filled
with the abundance
that is your season . . .

...the season of life...

...the season
of growth...

...a time when
the very earth
rejoices in the
wonder it is to
be alive.

May all of summer
remind you what
a joy you are to the world!

The birds that sing
for you ...

...the frogs that
jump for you...

...the bees that dance for you...

...and the river that roars with delight at the very mention of your name.

May all your days
burst with the joy
and color that are your
birthright to have:

The red of the hollyhock, to remind you to climb high.

The orange of the monarch,
to remind you to fly.

The yellow of the sun,
to remind you to smile.

The green of the
lily, to remind you
to be still.

The blue of the waterfall, to
remind you to wonder.

The violet of the
lavender, to remind
you to be true to the
royal within.

For you, child of
summer, are all that
is good, all that is bright,
all that is beautiful in
this vibrant time of year.

And that makes you special, indeed.

ABOUT BUSHEL & PECK BOOKS

Bushel & Peck Books is a children's publishing house with a special mission. Through our Book-for-Book Promise™, we donate one book to kids in need for every book we sell. Our beautiful books are given to kids through schools, libraries, local neighborhoods, shelters, nonprofits, and also to many selfless organizations that are working hard to make a difference. So thank you for purchasing this book! Because of you, another book will make its way into the hands of a child who needs it most.

If you liked this book, please leave a review online at your favorite retailer. Honest reviews spread the word about Bushel & Peck—and help us make better books, too!

NOMINATE A SCHOOL OR ORGANIZATION TO RECEIVE FREE BOOKS

Do you know a school, library, or organization that could use some free books for their kids? We'd love to help! Please fill out the nomination form on our website (see below), and we'll do everything we can to make something happen.

www.bushelandpeckbooks.com/pages/
nominate-a-school-or-organization

**BUSHEL
& PECK
BOOKS**

Published by Bushel & Peck Books, a family-run publishing house
in Fresno, California, that believes in uplifting children with the
highest standards of art, music, literature, and ideas. Find beautiful
books for gifted young minds at www.bushelandpeckbooks.com.

Type set in Aunt Mildred and IM Fell English Pro

Artwork licensed from Shutterstock.com

Bushel & Peck Books is dedicated to fighting illiteracy all over the
world. For every book we sell, we donate one to a child in need—
book for book. To nominate a school or organization to receive free
books, please visit www.bushelandpeckbooks.com.

ISBN: 9781638190011

First Edition

Printed in the United States

10 9 8 7 6 5 4 3 2 1

Printed in the United States
by Baker & Taylor Publisher Services